BUTTERFLIES IN PARIS

SHANNON O'CONNOR

CHAPTER ONE

"Come on! We're going to miss the train!" Sarah pulls my arm and I begrudgingly stand up. Who cares if we were a few minutes late anyway? We could always get the next one.

"Jeez, I'm coming." I stop looking at the crowds of people and instead start collecting my things. Sarah is not so patiently tapping her foot which kind of makes me want to go slower, but then Nick comes up behind her changing her tune completely.

"They didn't have the coffee you liked, but I got the French equivalent." Nick is Sarah's boyfriend, they have been dating for almost six years. Being high school sweethearts, and despite not going to the same college they stayed together.

"Oh my gosh! This is even better than the coffee back home!" She smiled taking a sip. Nick looked over and handed me a cup too.

"Mocha with no milk, just as you like." I smiled that he remembered my coffee order. I take it and silently notice how all of a sudden we're not in a rush.

"Come on B, we gotta go!" Sarah says as if reading my mind.

I put my camera back in its case and trail behind her and Nick. I had been trying to get a few photos of the inside of the airport. To anyone else, I'm sure it was just an airport, but to me, it was full of potential. Often the perfect shot could be found in a sea of people. I was in the middle of looking for it when Sarah started rushing me.

We have to find Leah and Tyler before we get on the train to the hotel. They said they were going to find a bathroom, but it was more likely they got distracted and were off kissing somewhere. Despite the seven-hour flight where they did not keep their hands off each other.

Sure enough, we find them kissing against a random wall on the way out of the airport. Sarah pulls them along and they follow behind me holding hands, stopping to look in each other's eyes.

I try to hold back my gags and eye rolls. Not everyone was as bitter as me. But then again they weren't the only single ones on a couples trip to *Paris*. They weren't the ones who just got dumped weeks earlier. Nope, they were happy, and in love, and Paris. Great for them.

I had tried to stay home, I tried to sell my ticket online so I could go to Mexico instead. But I had been so confident that I stupidly didn't get the insurance and my ticket to Paris was non-refundable. Sarah and Leah had promised that despite it being Paris, I wouldn't feel like a fifth wheel. But here we are ten hours into this trip and I couldn't feel more alone.

I'm attempting to tune them out, looking around at the people. We are standing inside the crowded airport, a variety of people, smells, and languages fill the air. It is mainly French I presume, but I haven't taken French in college like Sarah and Leah.

Tyler, Nick, Leah, and I wait to the side with our luggage while Sarah buys our train tickets. We are all grateful for Sarah's planning and taking charge abilities, without her there would be no trip. We used to joke that she was the mom of the group, always saving us from getting too drunk at parties or making sure we had a jacket on cool days. Now we like it.

I sip on my coffee and watch the people go to their destinations. The herds of people bustling through like Grand Central Station at peak time. I'm not out of my element with traveling, being from New York helps. I silently wish I had time to take out my camera, there are so many things I wanted to shoot. I knew I didn't have time so I settle on taking some photos on my phone. It was okay, not exactly what I wanted but it would do.

Sarah comes back with everyone's ticket and we follow her and Nick again. This time I trail behind everyone, not wanting to make it obvious how I am traveling with two other couples. I know it's dumb, but something about being here is only heightening the feelings of my breakup. It's only been a few weeks and this trip isn't making it any easier.

When we finally get to the hotel, all I want to do is a nap. I have no idea what time it is, and if that's even acceptable but I don't care. We all walk to our rooms and agree to meet up in an hour for dinner. Sarah thinks it would be cool to walk around the city at night after we have a nice dinner. Part of me doesn't want to go, but my growling stomach wins this time. I try to appreciate that I have a room to myself. When we booked this trip I thought Emily would be here with us.

I plop my bags on the floor and look around. The room isn't anything spectacular, we had all agreed we'd rather be closer to the Eiffel Tower than pay for a fancy hotel room. The walls are slightly chipped, and the bed doesn't look the most comfortable but it'll do. I plug in my camera with the universal wall plug Sarah insisted everyone buy. There's a small bathroom with an even smaller shower, at least everything looks clean.

I decide to shower, hoping that will wake me up but it doesn't seem to help. At least I got the gross airport feeling off me. I redo my hair and makeup and find an outfit I know will make me feel better. A soft pink dress that makes my curves look great, it also happened to be the dress I wore the night Emily and I met but I ignore that thought. I slide into it and recall Sarah had mentioned walking so I switch to my Doc Martens.

"Knock knock.," Sarah calls through the door. I walk over to let her in.

"Hey," I force a smile.

"Can we talk?" She looks serious so I nod and gesture to the bed. We both sit and it makes an unsettling sound.

"Well, thank God Emily's not here." I chuckle. Emily and I had never been able to keep our hands off each other and this bed would've been broken in minutes.

"That's actually what I wanted to talk to you about."

"Oh?" I avoid eye contact.

"I'm sorry if we started rough, I know this must be hard for you. And we told you to come, so I've talked to everyone and we're going to tone down the PDA." She smiles softly.

"S, it's okay you didn't have to do that." I feel bad now, I don't want to hold everyone back.

"It's not a big deal, we want you to have fun too. We didn't invite you like Emily's plus one, you're our best friend." She pulls me in for a hug and I smile. Her dark curls tickle my face but that's the hazard of her crazy beautiful hair.

I know she means well but I still feel bad. She had never been fond of Emily, to begin with, so her words aren't surprising. Besides, Sarah was my best friend. We had never had a best friend before each other. Coming into college was scary enough and having a random roommate was the worst. Sarah and I were paired up and I feared I'd spent the next year not speaking in my room but instead we became best friends. She was the bubbly outgoing type to my timidness, we balanced each other out.

Leah had transferred in our sophomore year of college becoming our next-door roommate. Bumping into each other in the halls had grown into a friendship. Tyler had been in my photography class, hitting on me only for us to become great friends when he learned I too liked girls. We had our own little close-knit friend group with others who came and went, but the five of us were strong. Even Nick had become more than *'Sarah's boyfriend'* over the years. He was someone I knew I could call a friend.

We walk downstairs to meet the group with my camera's travel bag slung over my shoulder. We are all walking in silence, too enamored by the beauty that is Paris. We could see the Eiffel Tower lit in the distance. I take out my camera and take a few shots, not stopping to see how they came out. We were all too starved to stop and I'd always have another chance to retake them.

At the restaurant, we sit outside and try not to look like tourists, but I'm sure our American accents give us away. Sarah and Leah explain the things on the menu we're unsure of while Tyler dares Nick to order escargot. Nick doesn't want to but the second Tyler calls him a chicken it's all over and Nick begrudgingly orders some. I order some crepes and we decide to split a bottle of champagne, after all, we are celebrating.

We'll be graduating college soon and entering the "real world". I'm going to take an internship in the city back home and hopefully get a job where I could take photos full time. Emily and I were going to get an apartment in the city together and maybe a cat too. Now I was going to have to find a roommate or something-

"Brooke!" Nick nudges me and I snap out of my thoughts.

"Yeah?" Everyone's looking at me with their glass of champagne in the air, I must have zoned out longer than I thought. I quickly grabbed my glass and put it up with theirs.

"As I was saying, I think this is going to be a great trip! Let's make the most of it." Sarah smiles, she and Leah take a few photos for Instagram before we can put our glasses down.

"My arm is killing me guys come on," Tyler complains after a minute.

"Oh yeah, Mr. Doesn't skip gym day I'm sure." Leah jokes and we all laugh.

Tyler could bench press Leah if he wanted to, he was all muscles and not afraid of showing them off. He rolls his eyes at Leah and she leans in to kiss him. I ignore the knots in my stomach, I should be happy for my friends. I try to remind myself of that over and over.

The waiter brings over the food, with Nick's food last. We all can't help but gawk at the way it looks, I try not to watch but the curiosity gets the best of me. Nick pokes at one with his fork while Tyler looks like he's going to be sick. Leah sticks to eating her pasta and I enjoy my crepes.

"You're going to make me sick! Just eat it!" Sarah complains. The way Nick's poking and prodding at it is worse than it looks.

"Oh come on you guys." Leah reaches over and grabs one off Nicks's plate surprising us all by eating it and not making a face. Our jaws drop while she goes back to eating her pasta.

"What?" She looks up.

"Holy shit! That's my girl!" Tyler boasts proudly and leans in for another kiss.

Not wanting to be outdone by a girl, Nick tries one and doesn't make a face either. Part of me wants to try one just out of curiosity but then again, they're snails. I'm not that curious.

"They taste like chicken," Nick says smiling. Sarah laughs and Tyler frowns that his dare hasn't gone to plan.

We all laugh and it's the first time I feel relaxed. I sip the champagne and devour the crepes until my plate is clean. Watching the lights on the Eiffel Tower and the nightlife of Paris in the background, makes me feel relieved I came.

Chapter Two

The next day Sarah wakes us all up early, insisting we need to stick to a schedule or we won't get to see everything. We walk to the Louvre, grabbing breakfast on the way to a cafe. A simple croissant and hot mocha put me in a good mood, which is important because I hate museums. I have never mentioned this to anyone, but I think they're a waste of time. Why do I want to walk through a building looking at old things I can't touch? Hint, I don't. But I don't want to miss out on the group activities so I don't bother mentioning it.

I take photos of everyone on the way. Taking candids while they grab a coffee, photos of Leah and Tyler kissing, the stolen glances Sarah and Nick give each other. Almost showing the different stages in relationships. Despite knowing each other for a while now, Leah and Tyler had only been dating eleven months, while Nick and Sarah were going on five and a half years. There was an unspoken familiarity and ease between Nick and Sarah while Leah and Tyler were still in their honeymoon phase.

The museum turned out to be boring, as expected. Although I did fake my "oohs" and "ahh's" perfectly. I took photos of everyone else while they took their Instagram photos, trying to get that perfect angle. Nick and Tyler stood to the side, knowing better than to get in the way of Leah and Sarah in Instagram mode. I chuckled, remembering the many times over the years we'd stop to get that perfect angle for them. They both managed to have quite a huge following for doing nothing over the years. But in theory, that's what Instagram is.

I start to feel like a fifth wheel by the end of lunch. Everyone is entangled in each other, holding hands and kissing while we walk the streets. I know they can't help it but it isn't helping how alone I feel. Part of me wants to stay back and explore on my own but I know Sarah would make a big deal of it. It's just hard watching everyone be so in love when that should be me. I should be as happy trailing behind and holding hands with Emily.

I think I would be handing everything better if there was some kind of warning, but Emily's breakup came out of nowhere. She had walked into my apartment off campus as she had most nights and asked to talk. We were only a week away from our Paris trip so I assumed she wanted to talk about that. *But as she pulled me into my room I could tell by the look on her face it was so much more than that.*

"I don't think I should go to Paris."

"What?" I was shocked.

"I don't think this is working anymore, and I don't want to string you along. So I don't think I should go to Paris." I sat on the edge of my bed as she stood in front of me. Her long brown hair was a curly mess around her face.

"W-What do you mean?" I didn't understand what she was saying. Where had this come from? I thought we were doing good, I was happy, wasn't she? My brain couldn't process anything, it was trying to wrap itself around her words.

"I'm sorry." She mutters. She bites her lip and looks at the ground avoiding eye contact with me.

"Are you...breaking up with me?" I was still unsure what this all meant.

"Yes, I think it would be for the best. You graduate soon, and I still have an extra semester I don't want to have to commute. I care

about you, and I just don't think this is working anymore." She walks over and before I can say anything else she kisses my forehead and disappears. The kiss lingers longer than she did.

I snap back into reality at the sound of Sarah's voice calling my name. She's twenty paces ahead with the group waiting for me. I catch up and try not to zone out again, it was hard not to see Emily everywhere. Part of me wondered what she ended up doing for spring break. I couldn't exactly ask or check-in, being mature we unfollowed each other and took a clean break despite how broken she left me.

After exploring the city for a few hours we all decided to head back to the hotel to regroup. I was thankful for the chance to rest, although my sneakers were comfortable I wasn't used to walking so many hours straight. We were all going to meet up in an hour to visit the Eiffel Tower. I made sure my camera battery was charged and ready for all the photos I would take from the top. It was something I was most excited about. I hoped the photos would distract me from all the couples.

Under Leah's advisement, we all dressed up for the occasion. I insisted on wearing my doc martens, my feet already had blisters from the day and I was told I'd be walking up many steps. Leah frowned at my shoes but knew better than to argue with me. Sarah had ordered our tickets ahead of time and despite the long lines, we were on our way up fairly quickly.

I took photos of the beautiful architecture, even the bottom of the Eiffel Tower was gorgeous. I stood underneath the middle of the tower and looked up, admiring the framework. We walked up what felt like thousands of steps, and I smiled silently to myself when Leah and Sarah complained about their feet. We first stopped at the first floor to look out at the view, then again at the second floor which was both amazing but the view at the top was breathtaking.

The sun was setting and the clouds were a variety of dark and light blues, the different hues creating a masterpiece in the sky. The city was lighting up for the night which included thousands of people who looked like ants from this view. It would be hard to describe to anyone who hasn't been, so I tried my best to take photos from every angle to capture its beauty. I knew I would be coming back during the day to capture a different view.

Sarah and Leah posed on the railing, looking over at the city while I took some shots. Then Leah stepped back giving Sarah a chance to take some photos herself. Nick stepped in behind her and I was going to grab some shots of both of them when he surprised us all by getting down on one knee. We all gasped in awe and I forced myself to take some photos, this was something they would not want to forget. Sarah turns around at our gasps and her eyes pop out of her head. Before she can say anything Nick pulls out a small box from his jacket pocket and starts to speak.

"Sarah, I never knew you would turn out to be the girl of my dreams. We met in high school and I thought you'd make a great prom date. But then I got to know you and fell in love. I fall more in love with you every day. You surprise me and make me a better version of myself. I would love to spend my life with you, traveling wherever you want to go, Sarah will you marry me?" He pops open the box and a beautiful oval-shaped diamond ring appears.

She has tears welling in the corners of her eyes and her hands are covering her mouth but she nods slightly. He stands up and before he can put the ring on her finger she wraps her arms around his neck. They kiss and I continue to grab photos of this life-changing moment. A small crowd of people has gathered nearby clapping and cheering. This may be the most cliche thing I've ever experienced and I have to ignore the feeling in my gut that is the opposite of how I should feel.

They stop kissing long enough for Sarah to put the ring on and I manage to take a few more photos. The crowd around them seems to disperse and they take a few moments by themselves. We walk away although it isn't fair for us to go, we try to give them some space.

"I can't believe they're engaged," Leah says with a huge smile.

"They deserve each other." It doesn't come out as sincere as I mean it but Leah and Tyler don't pick up on it.

"Now don't you get any ideas woman." Tyler chuckles embracing Leah.

"I mean maybe not in Paris, but when we graduate at our spot?" She laughs with him a smile as big as her face. He shakes his head and leans in to kiss her. They both seem to forget I'm there and as the kiss deepens I feel like I can't breathe.

"I'll be back." I push past them with the excuse of taking more photos but I just need some air.

Yes, we were outside but suddenly it was as if all the air was being sucked from my lungs. I felt so terrible, being so selfish but I couldn't fake it for a second longer. I just felt so alone, and it was only amplified spending time with them.

I walk back down to the second level giving me time to catch my breath. I'm about to take my camera off from around my neck to take a photo when someone bumps into my back. I turn around about to tell them to fuck off when I see her. My eyes lock with hers and suddenly all the rage from my body dissipates.

"Oh my gosh! I'm so sorry! I was trying to get out of the way and I didn't see you I'm so sorry!" She rambles and I can't help but smile at how adorable she is.

Her blonde hair is in a messy bun on the top of her head, leaving her blue eyes reflecting beautifully with the multicolored sky. She's wearing a loose white t-shirt and skinny jeans, but it's her shoes that catch my eyes. Her Doc Martens are identical to mine except hers contain several different colored paint splatters, and I'm in love. I look back up and realize she's waiting for me to say something.

"Do you not speak English? Parlez-vous français?" Her French is impeccable.

"I'm sorry, it's okay, I wasn't looking where I was going either." I smile.

"Oh, you're American! Thank goodness, my French isn't as good as it should be." She laughs. "I'm Willow." She extends her hand. Even her name was beautiful.

"Brooklyn, but everyone calls me Brooke." I shake it. I notice her extra short fingernails that are caked with paint and let my mind wander for a second.

"I like your shoes, Brooke." She winks and I have to remind myself not to read into it. There was no way I walked into a beautiful girl at the top of the Eiffel Tower and she was also into girls. That kind of thing didn't happen to me.

"Thanks..." I want to ask more but I don't even know what to say. Are you by some chance also into girls? I was so out of practice with something like this.

"Are you a photographer?" She eyes my camera. I think about how I would do anything to take her photo. She is stunning and to attempt to capture that on camera would be a dream.

"Yes, well not professionally, not yet. I graduate in a few weeks." I tend to ramble when I'm nervous.

"You should take my photo." She says boldly and smiles leaning against the railing to pose. She lets her blonde hair fall all around her face and I get a rush of the smell of strawberries.

I don't say anything but instead, pick up my camera and start to look for the perfect angle. I take a few photos as she giggles posing in different positions. I try to capture her laugh as best as I can. I notice she has blue and white paint smeared on the back of one of her arms and the side of her t-shirt. I wonder what she had been painting, she spoke perfect English but she didn't seem to be visiting. She turns and I grab a photo of the sun reflecting off her jawline, hoping it comes out just as magnificent as she looks. There is something about this girl I can't exactly put my finger on but she brings out a different side of me. I forget all about my friends and how sad I felt until I feel my phone buzzing in my bra. Since I didn't have a pocket in this dress I had to make do.

"Shit I have to check my phone." I pull it out to see several texts from Leah and the group chat. They were all looking for me. I shove my phone back into my bra.

"Do you have to go?" Suddenly Willow was inches from me, her bold eyes studying mine.

"I do, I'm sorry my best friend just got engaged and I kind of took off." I realize saying it out loud makes me sound even worse than I feel.

"A best friend you should be with?" I have to control my reaction, I know what she's asking me here.

"Oh no, just my best friend. But I was supposed to be here with my girlfriend and she dumped me a few weeks ago, and now I'm here with two other couples so it was just a bit much." I don't know why I'm divulging so much to a stranger but it just feels comfortable. And part of me is happy when I see the way she smiles when she hears I had a girlfriend.

"Well, if you want someone to take photos of again, you should call me."

She pulls a permanent marker out of her back pocket and grabs my hand. Her ice fingers send a chill down my arm. She scribbles her phone number - American - over the palm of my hand. I hold back a giggle even though the writing tickles. She turns before I can say anything more, walking around the bend and heading down the stairs. Before I can decide if I want to go after her, Sarah is calling my name from behind me.

"Dude where did you go? I didn't even get to show you my ring." She looks at me puzzled and I can see a million questions raising behind her eyes.

I clench my fist hiding the number. I don't know if she saw Willow or not but part of me wanted to keep this to myself. I didn't know if I would even call her, why shatter the dream right? But I knew I wanted to keep the memory of her intact.

"I'm sorry, I uh- wanted to get a shot before the sunset completely." I smiled. "Show me!" I add for good measure.

Sarah believes me and starts gushing about Nick and the ring.

We all agree it's impressive he pulled off such a huge surprise and we're all so glad she said yes. She goes into planning mode and rattles off all the things she'll have to do to plan the wedding. I'm only half-listening as my mind is still on Willow and the phone number that's burning a hole in my hand.

Chapter Three

We go out for drinks at a nearby bar to celebrate Nick and Sarah's engagement. We all do shots of vodka which only makes everyone more frisky. They can't seem to keep their hands off each other while I keep my hands on my drink. I chug two vodka cranberry and try to ignore how I feel. I know it isn't about me, so the drunker I get the easier that is.

I look around the crowded bar for someone like me, a third, well fifth wheel. Someone who just wants to go home and watch some Netflix, someone who wishes to be anywhere but here. But everyone here looks happy and drunk. Couples and friends and alike all buy drinks and celebrate things just like us.

I transferred Willow's phone number to my phone before we started drinking. I didn't know if I had the guts to call, but I knew drunk my might. I didn't want to make a fool of myself so I scrubbed the number best I could after adding it to my phone. Sarah was luckily too focused on her ring to notice when we stopped in the bathroom.

"So how long have you had the ring man?" Tyler asks Nick.

"Uh, actually a few months now," He looks embarrassed.

"What made you do it here and not at home?" Leah asks.

"I almost asked a few times back home, but my girl makes me

feel like I'm on top of the world. So I wanted to ask her when we were on top of the world."

"Oh my gosh, how did I get so lucky?" Sarah gushes and Leah aww's at his response. I try not to roll my eyes at the cliche response and finish off my drink. Everyone looks at me when the straw makes a sound against the ice in my cup.

"Damn, going for a new record there?" Tyler chuckles but I don't reply.

"I need another." I get up almost knocking the chair back and make my way to the bar.

A few people are sitting along the bar so I have to maneuver between them to get the bartender's attention. He's at the other end flirting with some brunette and I let my sigh out this time. Was it so hard to get a drink without having to witness another romance? I lean forward on the bar to brace myself, I'm feeling the effects of my drinks.

"Are you okay?" Nick's voice surprises me. He reaches out to steady my arm when I face him.

"I'm just trying to get another drink, but someone's too busy flirting," I say a little louder hoping the bartender will take a hint. He doesn't even glance in my direction.

"Are you sure that's a good idea? I know you're upset about things and maybe-"

"Don't try to act like you know how I'm feeling here Nick. Go back to your perfect little fiancé, drink your cheap whiskey, and let me get my damn drink." I snap, cutting him off. I was so sick of people thinking they knew what was best for me.

Nick looks stunned but he doesn't say anything else. I turn back to the bar while he goes back to the table. I consider reaching over the bar to get the drink myself. I could make a vodka cranberry faster than this moron would give me attention. Lucky for him, he finally notices me and walks over. He grabs my drink as quick as he can and heads back to the girl.

As I walk back to the table everyone is looking at me concerned. I frown, that is not the reaction I wanted. I decide I need some fresh air, instead of walking back to the table I throw back my drink and place my empty glass on a random table on the way out. I stumble a bit on the step at the exit but quickly regain my balance. The streets are uneven, all grey stones of different sizes. I walk as flat-footed as I can around the corner toward the hotel.

"BROOKE! BROOKE!" I can hear Leah's voice calling after me. I consider trying to run but I know I would fall before I could get anywhere.

"Yeah?" I call back and she appears in front of me.

"Dude, where are you going? We were waiting for you." She looks puzzled.

"I wanted to take a walk." I throw my arms in the air gesturing outside.

"You're drunk, and what you said to Nick was out of line. I know you're hurting because of Emily but that's no excuse-"

"Don't you start too Leah?" I roll my eyes and turn away from her lecture.

"Let's go, Brooke. We need to get back to the hotel." She tries to take my arm and I pull out of it. "Dude, what the hell?"

"I just want to take a freaking walk, let me go." She looks torn but ultimately lets me go with the agreement I'll be back soon.

I say yes to whatever to let her leave me alone and walk away. I walk along the streets under the dim lights. I make several turns and I'm probably lost but I don't care yet. The vodka has turned to a mellow buzz in my head. I think about going back to the hotel but I don't want to deal with anyone yet. It's all too much being here alone and that makes me think of Emily. Fuck Emily. She's the reason I'm having such a miserable time here. We should've been drunk on these streets together and instead, she left me.

I pull out my phone and scroll through my contacts looking for the right one. I put the phone to my ear and wait for her to pick it up. It rings a few times until she answers.

"Brooke?" She sounds sleepy. I forgot all about the time difference.

"Emily."

"Do you know what time it is? Are you alright?" I can hear her move around, maybe sitting up in bed. I try to picture her bed head and the way she looked in the mornings but it's harder to see.

"I-"

"Babe? Who is it?" I hear an unfamiliar voice on the other end. It takes a moment for me to realize that she must have someone else over. We broke up three weeks ago and she already had someone else in her bed?

"You're a bitch."

I WAKE up in the morning in my lumpy bed with a pounding headache and my mouth dryer than the desert. I move to sit up and realize there's someone in the bed next to me. My eyes widen at the sight of dark hair until I realize it's Leah. She snores and I look around the room spotting Tyler on the floor in a makeshift bed of pillows and blankets. Did they stay with me all night? When did I even get back to the room? How did I even get back to the room?

I try to think back to last night but everything is a blur. I can see a blur of Leah and Tyler helping me up the hotel stairs and into bed. I'm wearing a t-shirt that is a few sizes too big and doesn't belong to me. I notice it says *Yung Scuff* on it so it must belong to Tyler. I look for my phone but I don't see it on the nightstand so they must have it. I tiptoe to the bathroom for some water and maybe an aspirin. Tyler makes a sound as I walk past him but he doesn't wake.

I manage to drink three cups of water and find some spare Tylenol in my makeup bag. I look around the room for my phone but I don't see it anywhere obvious. I retreat to my side of the bed and getting back in wakes Leah.

"Hey," I say softly.

"Look who's up." She laughs as she sits up and stretches her arms over her head yawning.

"I'm sorry about last night, not that I remember it..."

"Well, aren't you lucky.?" She says with only a hint of sass.

"I'm not surprised, you outdrank us all," Tyler says from the floor.

"I'm sorry guys, what happened?"

"That'll be good." Tyler chuckles and Leah lets out a loud sigh.

Tyler climbs up to sit on the edge of the bed as Leah starts to tell me what happened last night. She relays the phone call with Emily, all the things I yelled at her, and how I almost threw my phone to the ground. How she had to confiscate it from me to protect it and how she and Tyler couldn't persuade me to go back to the hotel so Tyler ended up throwing me over his shoulder and carrying me the three blocks. Sarah and Nick were salvaging the rest of their engagement night and they took care of me. That included throwing up on my dress which is how I ended up in one of Tyler's T-shirts.

"We were worried you'd try to leave, so we stayed the night and hid your phone," Tyler adds.

"But how did you know where I was? I walked away from you guys after the bar." I ask confused.

"We were right behind you the entire time dude, we weren't letting your drunk ass go. You didn't want to hear it so you ignored anything we said." Leah laughs.

"Damn, I'm an asshole."

"Yeah, you were."

"I'm sorry, I'm sure I said some shit to you guys too and I'm sorry."

"We knew you were hurting but we didn't realize how much

dude. We care about you, you don't have to hide anything from us."

I just nodded not knowing what to say. I don't think I had realized how shitty I felt either. I suddenly remembered the words I spat at Nick and felt terrible. He didn't deserve any of that, especially on a day like yesterday. I felt like an ass. Tyler excuses himself back to their room to go shower, stopping to kiss Leah on the lips and leaving us alone.

"Here, I think you're sober enough for this." Leah reaches under her pillow and hands me my phone before getting up to use the bathroom.

I take it and notice a text on the home screen. Opening it I'm surprised to see a conversation started between me and Willow. I freeze afraid to read what the hell drunk me wrote knowing I probably ruined my chances of ever talking to her again. If only Leah could have taken my phone before I managed this. I take a breath and surprise myself by reading the texts.

'hey willow it is iI Brooke's

'HEY!:)'

'YOU HAVE the most beautiful eyes and ur photographic

'WOW, seems someone might be drunk. But thank you'

'CAN iI SEE YOU AGAIN?'

'MAYBE WHEN YOU'RE SOBER;)'

. . .

I notice in the message bar there's a text half typed out that I thankfully hadn't sent. That must have been when Leah took my phone from me. Let's just say if I had sent it that she might not have wanted to see me sober either.

"What's the damage?" She asks walking back from the bathroom.

"Well, I didn't get any angry texts from Emily."

"What about your French girl?" She raises an eyebrow at me and I quickly fumble over my words.

"Uh, what?"

"Oh come on, you had this goofy grin on and you kept talking about this beautiful French girl you met. With the *stunning blue eyes*." She imitates my voice at the end.

"It's nothing, I didn't say anything stupid. But I doubt it'll be anything." I shrugged trying to hide the excitement about her interest. I was sober and itching to message her back but I didn't know what to say.

"You deserve to be happy too to dude, even if it's only for spring break." She shrugs and heads back to her room.

I think about her words as I hold open my phone on the message thread with Willow. She wanted to see me again. So what was the harm? My heart was already broken, it's not like it could face any more damage with messaging her.

Chapter Four

We all meet in the lobby for brunch and I can tell Sarah's upset with me. She hasn't said anything about it, but she also hasn't said a word to me either. Knowing better than to keep trying I stay silent through brunch and give her time to cool off. I was kind of the worst drunk last night, I can't blame her for shutting me out. I manage to get Nick alone when Sarah, Leah, and Tyler go to the bathroom. It gives me a moment to apologize but he brushes it off.

"Don't worry about it, I know it was nothing personal. Just try to be nicer next time we drink, Sarah's still pretty pissed."

I just nod and everyone comes back moments before our food arrives. After brunch, Sarah surprisingly decides we should all go our separate ways. I'm sure it has something to do with me but I don't complain. Sarah and Nick take off to explore the city on their own while Tyler and Leah head back to the hotel room to 'make up for last night'. I had my camera with me so I decided to take a walk in the opposite direction of Sarah and Nick.

I checked my phone an embarrassing amount of times but there was still no text back from Willow. I'm not going to lie that bums me out but I try to ignore it. She was the idea of a spring break fantasy, I couldn't be upset over nothing. But as I looked at the photos we took yesterday I was hit with a twinge of sadness. I would've stayed longer and taken more photos if I had known I'd only get one chance.

I'm walking along with one of the side streets about to grab a cup of coffee when a bicycle comes out of nowhere running towards me, but as I fall backward out of the way, into the pavement someone catches me. Their strong hands grip my lower back and catch me just before my head hits the pavement. It was like that scene from *Twilight* only I was certain this time it wasn't a vampire who saved me. I brush the hair out of my face stunned to see my savior is none other than Willow. Attempting to regain my balance she helps me up and smiles.

"I know you're not used to the cyclists but you should be more careful." Her tone is careful, warning me, but not condescending. I notice a man running after his bicycle that almost hit me. I don't have time to process what just happened.

"I - uh I wasn't-" I stumble over my words shocked at our encounter. I pick up my camera bag and phone, checking both for damage thankful they were both in their cases.

"You were too busy texting me?" She laughs and I can feel the heat racing to my cheeks.

"Well, uh maybe," I admit. There's no use lying about it.

"I was just about to text back, ask if you wanted to meet up."

"You were?" I swear all my game left my body in my fall. I wasn't normally this much of a deer in headlights when I flirted.

"Why don't I buy you a cup of coffee and maybe give you a moment to get your words back?" She chuckles and I smile following her lead.

We each ordered our drinks; an iced mocha for me and an iced chai for her. I insist on paying since she saved my life and she unwillingly accepts. The person behind the counter says something in French and Willow translates that we can take a seat anywhere. We choose a table indoors, I'm partially scarred from my almost accident. The cafe has cute, black and white tile floors and a wall of roses perfect for any Instagrammer. It reminds me of a lot of the coffee shops back home in the city. I must have stumbled across a tourist spot.

As I sit down across from Willow I admire how beautiful she is. Her blonde hair is down today in loose waves that go just past her shoulders, her makeup is done lightly with purple eyeshadow and light pink lipstick, and she's wearing a floral skirt that ends just above her knee with a white cropped top to show off her chest. Not that I'm looking, but I may have checked her out. She's like something out of a magazine. I notice there's a streak of light blue paint on her ankle just above her sock line. It reminds me of yesterday and I wonder again what she might be painting.

"Are you okay?" She looks at me and I realize I've been staring at her feet. Oh my gosh, I probably look like some kind of a creeper with a foot fetish.

"I'm sorry, I'm not being weird, well maybe I am. But I noticed you had paint on your leg and you did yesterday so I was wondering what you were painting." I ramble and she laughs again. Light and airy.

"It's okay, a hazard of the job for sure. I'm an artist. I'm working on a mural right now so I tend to have paint on me. Even when I think I've got it all." She smiles and glances at the spot and shrugs, A waitress brings over our drinks and places them in front of us.

"What is the mural for?" I ask sipping on my drink.

"It's for a new restaurant actually, they're opening in a month and wanted something that would attract customers."

"Wow, so you must be pretty good." I was way out of my league here.

"I do okay, I did a smaller painting for a friend of theirs and they loved it so much they reached out." She's proud but humble.

"That's so amazing, what is it going to be?"

"Do you want to see it?" She looks at the time on her Apple watch and frowns. "It's across town but I have to be there soon anyway."

"I'd love that."

She smiles and puts her hand out for me to grab. Her thin long fingers have paint under the unpolished nails and they are cold. Despite it being almost 75 today her hands are freezing. I try not to make a big deal of this as my stomach is doing somersaults and I know I'm blushing more than the red top I'm wearing. Thankfully I was looking somewhat cute in my jeans and a loose t-shirt. I would have dressed up more if I had known I'd be going on an adventure with this French goddess.

Willow and I walk to the bus a few blocks away and she helps me pay the fare. I had stuck to using my credit card for things, not wanting to bother with exchange rates and foreign money.

"Are you from here?" I finally ask. I know it sounds rude but I've been trying to figure it out all day.

"I'm not. I'm actually originally from the States, but I haven't been in years. I spent time in London, then Germany, now Paris. I'm not sure how much longer I'll be here though."

"What makes you think that?" Everything about her is interesting.

"I like to travel and paint and when I'm done with a few pieces I move to find more inspiration." She smiles and I can see the light in her eyes. The need to find more in the world, the want, the desire to find meaning in it all. It's something I have seen in countless other artists, but she was impressing us all by actually doing it.

"I wish I could do that, with photography," I admit. There's something safe about her.

"Why can't you?" Before I can answer the bus stops and she jumps up "Shit! This is us! Stop!"

She grabs my hand and pulls me with her to get off the bus. She laughs as we make it to our stop by half a second. Luckily the driver heard us running to get off and gave us a chance to catch up. I look up at a large empty storefront, the windows covered up with newspaper. There's a large red awning that looks brand new and a spot for the restaurant name to be but it's empty.

"Come on."

She takes my hand in hers again and pulls me forward to the doors. She pulls out a keyring of keys from her bag and unlocks the front door. She leads me in first and I realize now that she could be about to kidnap the dumb American tourist because I followed a pretty girl to an abandoned site without telling my friends. Part of me wishes I had told someone I even left the city but I was so distracted it didn't cross my mind.

"Does anyone know you're here?" She asks suddenly as if reading my mind. My eyes go wide as I'm unsure how to reply. "I'm not going to kill you, I just wanted to know if you needed the address to tell your friends."

"Oh, yeah that would be good. Thanks." I feel better after texting Leah and updating her as vaguely as I can about where I am.

"Do you always follow strangers to strange locations?" She laughs at me.

"Only the pretty ones," I smirk. Maybe all my game wasn't lost after all.

She rolls her eyes smiling and leads me to the basement of the place. It's dark so she tells me to wait by the stairs while she grabs the lights. After about a minute the lights slowly flicker on illuminating the entire basement. There are chairs and tables folded up in not corner but besides that the basement is empty. I look around and see the mural she must be working on.

On the far right corner, there is a beautiful painting of a sky with clouds and flowers, all in shades of the blues I've seen on Willow. The sky continues to the next wall where there's half a painting of a beautiful woman. Her outline is done with amazing curves, long flowing thick curls and she looks like an angel. Even unfinished, it's breathtaking.

"I'm not done yet, hopefully soon but I was having trouble with what to do on that wall." Willow comes back explaining and points to the wall on the opposite side of us. It's painted the same base as the other walls and it has a few clouds sharing from the completed wall but nothing else.

I don't say anything but a step closer to the mural taking it all in. As I get closer I realize there are words lightly painted into the clouds and smaller things painted into the flowers. It had more depth than I originally thought.

"Are you okay if I work on it? Or do you need to get back?"

"I can stay, can I take some photos?"

"Only if they're of me." She winks and disappears again. I pull out my camera and look for the perfect angle of the mural. I want to be able to capture it fully to show everyone. I know it's not the same but it is so beautiful.

Willow emerges a few minutes later completely changed into a long t-shirt and an extra-large white button-down that doubles as a smock. Both are covered in paint from the mural. Her hair is piled in a small bun on the top of her head and she is carrying a sketchbook over to one side of the mural. She pulls a pencil out of the tiny bike shorts she's wearing under the t-shirt and adds to a sketch in the book. After a few minutes, she puts the book down and starts to open the paints. She lays down a white tarp and lays out the brushes and colors she needs.

"You can come closer." She smiles.

I take off my shoes to follow Willow's lead and put them down near the stairs walking closer to her with my camera. She's fully into painting mode and doesn't seem to pay me any more attention. She's mixing colors and I start to take photos. The way she looks so determined and calm at the same time is amazing to capture. She bites her bottom lip as she picks up one of the brushes dragging it across the wall to add some color to the woman. I watch in awe through my lens as she makes everything look so effortless.

I snap away as she brings the woman to life with color. My focus changed from Willow to the mural and back again. It was hard not to admire the way the mural brought out the blue in her eyes and the paint she had along her cheekbones. I can see how she always ended up with paint on her; she uses her hands to fix a piece and forgets it's there leaving a trail of paint along her body.

I'm so into the photos that I'm taking that as I walk around I'm completely unaware of my surroundings until I step right into a puddle of paint and fall backward. Hearing the disaster I made Willow turns around shocked to find me laying on my back with white paint covering most of me. Luckily at the last second, I tossed my camera to the side, wanting to save it from the paint.

"You don't know how to be careful do you?" She cracks herself up as she takes a moment to take it all in.

"A little help here would be nice, I can feel it going into my underwear," I complain. I didn't know how to begin to get up, everywhere was paint.

"Here," She says as she puts down her brush.

She walks over to me, putting out her hand to help me up. I grab on and she can pull me slightly but her feet give out and we are both falling this time. She falls directly on top of me. I caught her body pulling it into mine, my hands resting on her hips while hers landed on my chest. Some of her hair is falling out of her bun into her face and she scrunches her nose.

She doesn't say anything as I lift one hand to push the blonde hair behind her ear. I forget my hands are covered in paint and I accidentally leave behind a trail of white on her face. She doesn't break eye contact as she bites her lip hesitantly and I can see the lust in her eyes. I don't hesitate to lean in, putting my hand behind her neck and pulling her in for a kiss.

It is unlike any kiss I've had before. We are ravenous, unable to keep our hands off each other. We kiss with our hands moving in every direction, not caring what kind of a mess we are creating. We lose ourselves in each other becoming our masterpiece.

Chapter Five

Willow and I lay entangled with the paint drying all over us. We both look like a painting in progress but we don't say anything. Her head is laying on my bare chest as I run my fingers through her hair. We both lay in a different spot on the tarp, our clothes in a pile near us while we look up at the mural. She looks calm as she looks at it now as if she's finally found the last piece of a puzzle.

I don't want to move, or leave this spot, being here with Willow feels safe. I know how that must sound, I feel safe with a stranger. I've known her for less than twenty-four hours and yet I felt so at peace here. I didn't know what this was, or where it was going-if anywhere-but for once I didn't care.

"Is that you?" Willow looks up confused pulling me from my thoughts. I realize she's asking about the buzzing and I realize it must be my phone.

"Ugh, yeah it must be one of my friends." I moan. I did not want to give up Willow's warmth for the cold comments from my friends.

"You should get it, in case they're worried."

I nod knowing she's right. I don't want them to be stressed. I caused enough of that last night. Willow lays back moving off my chest while I walk over to our clothes looking for my phone in the pocket of my jeans. It's still buzzing when I get to it, Leah's calling.

"Hey."

"Dude! What the hell?!" She exclaims.

"What?"

"You text me some sketchy address and that you're with some strange girl in a foreign country like it's nothing? We were worried."

"Shit, I'm sorry. I told you where I was. I didn't have my ringer on so I lost track of time." I glance at the time on my phone and frown. We had been gone for hours, it was almost 6:30 pm.

"We're just glad you're okay, are you coming back for dinner?"

"Uh..." My voice trails as I look back at Willow. It was hard enough getting up for this phone call, I didn't want to leave her right now.

"We're finishing up shopping and we're going to pick up the guys for dinner. I take it things are going well." I quickly press down the volume button hoping Willow isn't listening. I'm standing completely naked five feet away but for some reason, I'm blushing like an idiot.

"Uh yeah, I'll try to meet you guys," I say ignoring her comment. She laughs and says okay hanging up with the agreement that I'll share my location with her until I get back to the hotel.

"Everything good?" Willow's standing behind me reaching to touch my waist. I turn around pushing my body against hers and lean in to kiss her. Her soft lips taste like the coffee we drank and leftover paint. Despite the aftertaste, I love kissing her.

"Everything's great," I smile pulling away from the kiss.

"Why don't I bring you back to the hotel so you can clean up?" She bites her lip and looks at me. "We can get dinner after?" She suggests after sensing my hesitation of saying goodbye.

"Mmm," I respond leaning back to kiss her.

We kiss for a few more moments but we both know we'll be back on the floor if we continue, so we unwillingly part and get dressed. Getting dressed with dry paint on your body and dry paint on your clothes is not an easy task. Parts of you are sticky and other parts feel like sandpaper as the clothes rub.

I check on my camera, thankful that once again it didn't have any damage. There was a small splash of white paint on the neck strap but otherwise, it didn't seem to be too bad. Willow disappears in the back again and returns in her clean clothes from earlier. Despite the clothes, you can see the paint all up and down her legs, including a few handprints of mine pretty high up her thighs. I blush as she catches my stare.

"I'm sorry I don't have any other clothes here for you." She frowns.

"It's okay, I'm sure we'll get plenty of looks though."

"That's only because you're so beautiful." She leans in close and brushes my lips.

It's enough to drive me wild, but before I can pull her in for a longer kiss she's running up the stairs. I grab my camera and chase after her, that lip bite will be the death of me. I finally catch up to her at the front doors so I push her against them, lightly, watching her eyes grow wide in anticipation. I lean in to kiss her but instead lean in close, and leave soft kisses down her jaw to her neck. She moans softly in my ear and I pull away laughing.

"Well, let's go." I chuckle.

Her jaw drops as she attempts to compose herself. She shoots me a look that tells me I'll be paying for that later. I follow her back to the bus stop and as we board a few minutes later we get looks from everyone. She keeps her eyes on me as we grab two seats in the back. I place my hand on her thigh and she keeps her eyes on me.

The sun is setting behind her and I can't help myself. I have to take a photo of this. She doesn't protest instead slightly posing for me. She stops posing and looks at me suddenly. It's chilling, she's looking right past the camera at me and I have to remember to breathe. I can see the kindness in her eyes, a sense of serenity flows through me. She smiles slightly and I notice that she has a small dimple. I had missed it before but now there was no way to unsee it. I was quickly learning so much about her.

32

Chapter Six

Willow and I get off the bus a few blocks from the hotel. Sarah and Leah text me asking if I want to meet them for dinner. After they spent the day with Nick and Tyler they went shopping together, something they knew I'd have no interest in. I'm silently thankful, I was not a fan of shopping all day long that sounded like a drag. I text that I'm stopping at the hotel but I can meet them in a half-hour or so. I need time to get all the paint off me.

We take the elevator up ignoring the looks of the other guests as we walk through the hotel. I'm positive we look insane so no one dares to say anything. We kiss in the elevator until it stops a floor below ours. We pull apart and to my surprise it's Nick.

"Brooke?"

"Nick!" I smile. He looks me up and down then at Willow, raising an eyebrow.

"Do I wanna ask?" He chuckles.

"A story for another day, but this is Willow." I blush as I introduce them. They nod to each other instead of shaking hands and the elevator brings us to our floor.

"What brings you back?" I ask Nick.

"I was going to meet up with Sarah and Leah for dinner but I forgot my wallet so I had to come back."

"If you don't mind waiting I'm going to go too."

"Yeah no worries, I'll be in the room then. I assume you need to shower." He cracks a smile.

"Whatever makes you think that?" I say sarcastically.

Nick heads to his room to wait while I lead Willow to my room. We both get undressed and head inside the bathroom, I turn on the shower to get warm and we both jump in. There's barely enough room for both of us but we make it work. Switching between kissing and shampooing, kissing and getting clean, after some good scrubbing we do manage to get the paint off.

Willow changes back into her clean clothes while I search for a new pair of jeans and a shirt to wear. I settle on a loose tank top and my motorcycle jacket, my small attempt at dressing up for dinner. I run a brush through my hair a few times and grab my Doc Martens. I'm about to ask Willow if she wants to join us for dinner when my phone rings.

'has anyone heard from Tyler- L'

'GUYS! i'm actually worried, it's been hours- L'

'COULD YOU CHECK ON HIM PLEASE?- L'

I LET her know I'll check on him and put my shoes on. He's notorious for going to the gym and napping after so maybe he's just sleeping. Normally he's pretty quick to answer Leah's texts and calls, knowing of her heightened anxiety.

"I just have to check on my friend, but would you like to come to dinner with me and my friends?" I smile.

"Sure," Her answer surprises me but I don't complain.

Willow and I walk down the hall to Tyler and Leah's room. I'm surprised to find Nick on his way there too.

"Sarah asked if I could check on him, just in case he was sleeping nude or something." Nick chuckles. Tyler often boasted about sleeping naked, something about letting everything breathe.

We reach Tyler's door a few steps later but the sounds inside make us freeze. Willow looks confused waiting for us to move, but Nick and I are frozen in place. Coming from inside Tyler's rooms are moans and sounds I know all too well from Tyler's overnight visits with Leah. Only Leah's moans weren't coming from behind that door, it was someone else.

"He's not." I choke out. He wouldn't do that to Leah, especially not in Paris.

"What's happening?" Willow whispers.

"We should go," Nick shakes his head.

"What? No, if he has a girl in there we have to be sure." I ignore Nick and I knock loudly on his door. The sounds stop and I can hear movement.

"Hello?" Tyler calls out after a moment.

"It's Brooke!" I call back. I can hear more movement inside, some low voices, and then Tyler appears at the door.

"Hey, what's up?" Tyler looks ruffled, his hair is a mess and his t-shirt and khakis are wrinkly. He only opens the door enough to stand in the doorway, his hand holding it steady.

"Uh, Leah was looking for you. We're going to meet her and Sarah for dinner." Nick says.

"Oh, uh okay. Maybe I'll just meet you there? I have to change." He looks nervous and I try not to give it away that we know. I'm hoping so much that I'm wrong.

"Okay." Nick smiles and Tyler closes the door slowly.

"What just happened?" Willow whispers again.

"Shh come on!" I grab her hand and pull her down the hall. Nick follows silently behind confused.

I lead them both toward the elevator where we can hide

behind a nearby plant. If Tyler does have someone in there she'll have to leave by this elevator and then we'll know for sure. I whisper my plan to Nick and Willow, but just before Nick can protest we hear Tyler's voice. We hide as we watch Tyler lead a redhead down the hall and onto the elevator. He presses the button looking around nervously, then she kisses him. They're too entangled in each other to notice so I take out my phone and grab a few photos. If we have to tell Leah about this then I need to have some sort of proof. They pull apart and the woman walks into the elevator as Tyler goes back down the hall to his room.

"Tyler's cheating on Leah," I say shocked. Willow looks confused but she doesn't say anything letting us have a moment.

"It's not our business Brooke." Nick shakes his head.

"What are you talking about Nick? We have to go tell Leah."

"You want to ruin this whole trip? Why would you tell her?" Nick snaps.

"You can't be serious," Willow says causing Nick and me to look at her shocked. "I'm sorry," she mumbles.

"She's right Nick, Leah is our friend. What Tyler did is wrong." I push the button on the elevator and take Willow's hand.

"Just wait until we get home Brooke, what's the rush?" Nick asks as we get in the elevator.

I'm silent as I consider it, I guess there is no rush. As much as I want to tell Leah I know that it would ruin the trip for everyone. She doesn't deserve to have her spring break ruined because Tyler couldn't keep his hands to himself. I want to be surprised but this isn't exactly out of character for him. He's always had a wandering eye, being flirty with everyone, but I thought that was its extent. I never thought he'd make a move and cheat on her.

We all stay silent the rest of the elevator ride. I fight with myself internally struggling to figure out the right thing to do. All I know is, I wish I didn't go on this stupid trip to Paris.

Chapter Seven

Willow hits it off with Sarah and Leah almost immediately. They bond over their love of the office, mozzarella sticks, and museums. Three things I absolutely despise. It takes some of the pressure off me, which gives me time to think. Willow's hand is on my thigh with her thumb rubbing back and forth hopefully giving me a sense of serenity.

We were sitting in a fairly nice restaurant eating some of the best pasta I've ever had. We all ordered drinks and shared some appetizers, which is how my distaste for mozzarella sticks came up. I didn't see the point in eating a cheese stick deep fried in bread when there were much better appetizer choices.

Tyler showed up fifteen minutes after we did, in a new outfit and newly showered. He kissed Leah hello and acted like he wasn't fucking another girl less than an hour ago. Nick looks even calmer than Tyler like he didn't even care his best friend was hurting someone we all care about. The whole situation was making me sick to my stomach.

"B?" Sarah saying my name brings me back to the table.

"Sorry what?" I wasn't paying attention.

"Willow said she wanted to take us to this dessert place she knows nearby." Sarah smiles.

"Oh, that sounds good." I smile back at her.

"Let me go pay." Nick takes the check with all our cards and heads to the front to pay. Tyler excuses himself to go to the bathroom and I give myself a second to breathe.

"You guys are so cute, I can't believe you met on the Eiffel Tower! That's like the ultimate meet-cute." Sarah gushes. She was all about the romance and cliches that come along with them.

"Well, we wouldn't have met if she wasn't so clumsy." Willow chuckles.

"We should take a photo of you guys!" Sarah exclaims.

"Oh no, I'm behind the camera not the one who gets photographed." I protest.

"Well, I would love my photo taken." Willow starts to pose.

"Here Leah you take them, you're better at this than I am." Sarah picks up my phone off the table and hands it to Leah. We all know each other's passcodes, never having anything to hide from each other.

"Smile, for me?" Willow smiles at me hopefully and I can't deny this.

This could be the first and only photo I'll get to have of us. I smile and she surprises me by pulling my face in to kiss me. This girl was full of surprises. Sarah and Leah "Ewwww" from the other side of the table.

"Okay, let's see how they came out." Leah starts scrolling through the photos with Sarah looking over her shoulder.

I'm still coming down from the high of kissing Willow again when I remember the photo I took earlier; of Tyler kissing someone else. I go to grab my phone from Leah but I know it's too late.

"W-What is this?" She turns the phone around to show me the photo I was worried about.

"Leah I'm so sorry-" I'm cut off by Nick and Tyler coming back to the table.

"Ready to go?" Tyler smiles at her.

Everyone else is silent as she holds the phone up. Nick's eyes go wide shooting me a look but I am frozen. No one knows what to do or say.

"What is this Tyler?" She turns the phone toward him and he pales instantly.

"I- uh," He's at a loss for words too.

"Brooke, please tell me this is a joke." Leah has tears pouring down her cheeks.

"I'm sorry, I wanted to tell you. Nick thought-"

"YOU KNEW?!" Sarah cuts me off this time to yell at Nick.

"Well, yeah." He looks down but I can tell this is what he was trying to avoid.

"You knew my best friend was getting cheated on and you didn't say a word?" Sarah is angry and although she isn't yelling her voice carries, causing people at nearby tables to look.

"How could you do this?" Leah asks Tyler now. She stares at him broken, and by the look in her eyes, I can tell that's how she feels. No one can describe the pain of being cheated on by someone you truly love.

"It was only-" Tyler is interrupted again.

"Don't you DARE SAY IT WAS ONLY ONE TIME," Leah yells.

"Maybe we should take this outside," Sarah whispers to Leah.

"Fine." She drops my phone on the table and storms out.

"This is exactly what I didn't want Brooke." Nick spits.

"This is not Brooke's fault Nick. She absolutely should tell her best friend what a sack of crap he is for cheating on her with some French bimbo." Sarah yells and follows after Leah.

Tyler is the only one to stay silent and unmoving. He hasn't sat down or taken any steps outside either. I think he's not sure what to do. Willow picks up my phone and hands it to me but I'm only half paying attention. I feel like everything and everyone is moving around me but I'm frozen. I can tell Willow is waiting for me to say or do something. Nick leaves to find Sarah and Tyler looks up at me with pleading eyes. Part of me wants to feel bad for him.

"Let's go," Willow holds out her hand taking charge.

She leads us out of the restaurant and I look around for my friends. Sarah and Nick are comforting Leah but she's sobbing into Sarah's shirt. They don't notice us walk out so Willow leads us down the opposite way.

"I figured you could use a moment to breathe."

"Thank you, I'm so sorry about this. I never expected-"

"Hey, it's okay. It's not your fault your friend cheated on his girlfriend and your other friend asked you to cover it up. It's a terrible situation." She rubs my shoulders and pulls me in for a hug.

"Do you think we could meet up tomorrow? I just need to be with my friends tonight." I frown.

"Of course, why don't I pick you up to say noon? We can have a picnic." She smiles and leans in to kiss me. I melt into her touch once again.

"Brooke!" I hear my name call and pull away from Willow. She touches my cheek and I close my eyes smiling.

We depart without another word and I turn around to my friends. To hopefully salvage our relationships and the rest of this trip.

Chapter Eight

The next morning I wake up to the sound of snoring in my face. I open one eye seeing Leah in front of me. Her morning breath and all, snoring loud as can be. I lean away from her, laying on my back and recalling last night. Sarah was on Leah's other side sleeping soundly, she was more used to Leah's snoring than I was.

They had both fallen asleep last night in my room bed last night. After Willow left everything was a complete disaster. Leah was angry with Tyler for cheating and angry with me for not telling her, Sarah was angry with Nick for trying to hide it from Leah, and Nick and Tyler were somehow both angry with me. After some arguing, Leah calmed down enough to realize she wasn't angry with me and understood it was a difficult situation for anyone to be in. So Sarah, Leah, and I went back to the hotel drank cheap wine, and fell asleep watching Netflix on my laptop.

I open my phone and see a text from Willow saying she's on her way. It's 11:14 and I had 45 minutes to shower and be ready. I was nervous and excited all at once at the thought of spending the day with Willow again. I only hoped my friends wouldn't give me any trouble about going.

I sneak out of bed not waking either of them and head to the shower. When I get out I ruffle around in my suitcase with one hand on my towel. I'm trying not to wake them but I also don't want to leave without them knowing I'm gone. I go back to the bathroom to get dressed and am happily surprised Sarah's awake when I get back.

"Hey, how are you?"

"Exhausted, hungover I think." She takes a long sip from her water bottle on the nightstand. Her brown hair is ruffled from the night, it was unusual not to see her put together by now.

"Are you going to talk to Nick?" I walk over and sit on the edge of the bed. She's playing with her engagement ring frowning.

"I mean yeah, I kind of have to. But it's just like he thought what Tyler did was okay? He's okay with him cheating on my best friend and then trying to get you to keep it a secret?"

"He was always going to tell Leah, he just didn't want the trip ruined. In a way I got it, I was struggling with it myself when I found out. But Nick is a good guy, he loves you so much, you should at least hear him out." I smile and she nods.

"Are you going out?" Leah turns over in bed looking at us.

"Uh well, Willow invited me to a picnic. But if you need me I don't have to go..."

"No no, it's good. She seems great and you should enjoy yourself." She smiles at me. "Sarah, can we get drunk at Disneyland Paris?"

"Hell fucking yeah!" Sarah cheers. I was happy they weren't going to spend all day in bed wallowing, and I definitely wasn't sad about missing that. Disneyland Paris was fun, but if I had to choose between that and Willow, I'd choose Willow every time.

I finish getting ready while they talk about what they should wear. I throw on a little makeup as a change and make sure I grab my camera's extra battery. Something tells me I'm going to be taking lots of photos today.

I meet Willow downstairs ten minutes later and she's two minutes early waiting for me with flowers. She's wearing a beautiful floral pink sundress, white sneakers, and holding an oversized bag I assume is a makeshift picnic basket. Sticking out of it is a very large baguette. She embraces me with a kiss on the cheek and takes my hand in hers.

"How was your night?" She asks.

"Oh you know, super fun," I say sarcastically.

"Well, hopefully, today takes your mind off things."

She leads us down a few blocks and I don't pay attention to where because at this point I'm sure she's not a murderer. We arrive at the back of the Eiffel Tower, or maybe it's the front, I honestly can't tell. She pulls a thin white sheet from her bag and lays it on the grass. I offer to help set up but she says she has it covered so I take a few photos of the Eiffel Tower while I wait. She sets up some sandwiches, a bottle of champagne, and some fruit, along with the baguette. Everything looks picture perfect and I am starving. She tells me I can sit and she hands me a plastic glass which she fills with champagne, then pours herself a glass.

"A toast, to chance meetings" she smiles. We clink glasses and each takes a sip.

She tells me all about the places she's been, the people she's met, and the things she's painted. She says London was her favorite so far, she thrives better in cities and London gave her the chance to meet more people than here. She tells me that once this mural is done she's moving on, most likely Spain. She's been learning Spanish just as she learned French before coming to France. She tells me how she's immersed herself here and that's what she tries to do in each new place.

The more she tells me about everything is the more I'm in awe. She's only a few years older than I am, and already she's experienced and lived so much. She opted out of college and that seems to have made the biggest difference for her career. Although she travels a lot, most of it is paid for by the pieces she creates.

"You're incredible," I smile at her. We're both on our third glass of champagne and despite the food, I'm feeling it.

I lean in to kiss her and lose my hands in her hair. The blond curls are smooth as butter slipping through my fingers. She places a hand on my cheek and I lean into it, losing myself to her touch. She pulls away smiling and blushing just as the kiss gets heated.

I understand her hesitation, there are a lot of people nearby. A lot of other couples on romantic picnics, older couples with their children, and grandparents too old to sit on the grass, but having picnic on some of the benches. Everyone is in their own world, enjoying the view, but lost in who they're with. I snap a few photos of strangers, the Tower, and the magnificent view.

"Are you going to take my photo?" Willow throws back her champagne and giggles with me.

"I thought you'd never ask." I chuckle and point the camera at her.

I zoom out so I don't end up with a photo of her nose. Sometimes I end up taking better photos when I'm a little buzzed because I don't overthink it as much. Willow stars posing, throwing her head back with laughter, making silly faces, and then just smiling at me. I laugh with her, feeling blissful at this moment with her.

She crawls over to me to look at them together. She lays in my arms with her head on her chest, arms wrapped around her as I click through the photos. She tells me which are her favorites and asks me to send them to her later. I nod and kiss her forehead. I feel a sudden sense of sadness, soon this will be ending. Not just this trip, but having Willow in my arms, being able to kiss her, being with her like this. I push the thought out of my head as quickly as I can. This isn't the time to worry about something like that, something I can't control. I need to enjoy this moment for as long as I can.

Willow and I spend the next few hours in each other's arms. We finish the bottle of champagne and I feed her grapes. I tell her about my life back home and she is interested when I speak. I tell her about the plan I have for after I graduate; moving to the city and interning until I get a job. My plans seem small compared to hers but she doesn't judge them.

When the sun starts to set we realize we've been gone all day. I check my phone and am relieved to see Nick joined Sarah and Leah at Disneyland Paris. Tyler isn't in any of the photos and I silently wonder what he's up to. I also wonder what the hell got into his head to do something like that. Whatever, it wasn't my business.

Willow and I decided to head back to the hotel before dinner so we start to clean up the picnic. I'm picking up my camera off the ground when I feel something land on my nose. I cross my eyes to see it before making any moves in case it was a bee, but to my surprise, it's a butterfly. Willow's eyes go wide as she notices.

"Hold still!" Willow grabs the camera out of my hands as quickly as she can without moving me.

I don't say anything because I'm afraid I'll scare it away, but the butterfly stays on the bridge of my nose. Its wings look like a painting, unique and beautiful. It flutters its wings, tickling my nose but I still don't move. Willow takes photos of the butterfly and I try to smile without moving my face. I'm trying not to breathe too heavily which is not the easiest under pressure. After a moment the butterfly takes off toward the tower and I can breathe again.

"Wow, that was amazing." She smiles looking over the photos. I look over her shoulder and am amazed at the photos she captured.

"Those look great," I gush.

"That's all you, and the *Mariposa*,"

"The what?" I look at her confused.

"Sorry, Mariposa is Spanish for butterfly. It's funny because I just learned that word a few days ago." She chuckles for a second and then she furrows her brow.

She stays silent as we finish cleaning up the picnic. We throw away the garbage and pack up her sheet and the containers from the food. She takes my hand as we walk back to my hotel but she doesn't say another word. It's unlike her but I don't push it as I try to think of anything I could have said wrong.

"Hey I actually have to go, but I'll text you okay?" Willow says as we get to my hotel. She gives me a quick kiss and before I can reply she's headed down the street.

I try not to read into it as I get in the elevator and end up in my room. I thought we had a good day, was I wrong? Her abrupt goodbye had me overthinking everything. I sigh change into some pj's and settle into watching a movie on my computer. Sarah, Nick, and Leah were still at Disneyland so I would be on my own for dinner. I wasn't that hungry so I stuck to the chips I had gotten on the plane and some other snacks I had brought back to the room. Although I tried distracting myself with a movie, the only thing on my mind was Willow.

Chapter Nine

I wake to my phone ringing the next morning jolting me awake. What time was it? I remember seeing my friends, talking to them for hours, and hearing about their adventure until we all went our separate ways. Leah ended up staying the night in my bed again, it made the most sense since she hadn't bothered talking to Tyler yet. But my phone is ringing so I reach for it surprised to see Willow's name.

"Willow? What time is it?" I ask groggily.

"Seven-ish, I think. I know it's early,"

"Are you okay? What's going on?" I sit up suddenly anxious.

"Nothing, actually I was wondering if you could come to meet me? I have something I want to show you."

"It couldn't wait?" I chuckle as I yawn.

"No, trust me I waited until seven." She laughs and I can't help but smile.

"Text me the address, I just need to get dressed."

"Okay! Bring your camera!" She says excitedly and hangs up.

"Everything okay? What time is it?" Leah looks up at me. I hadn't meant to wake her.

"Yeah, sorry Willow wants me to meet her."

"At Seven am?" Leah squints at her phone. "Have fun on your booty call."

"It's not a booty call oh my gosh." I shake my head as I pick out clothes.

"Uh-huh, okaaaaay," She turns back over to fall asleep.

I don't think it's a booty call, she would've just said so, right? With Leah's comment in my head, I choose a bra and matching panties under my simple black t-shirt and jeans. I look at my phone as I head get in the elevator, I consider taking a bus but I don't want to get lost so I settle for a cab. I read off the address and as he drives I text Sarah letting her know where I'm going. I'm sure she's not awake yet but I figured Leah was too sleepy to recall any important details.

Twenty minutes later the cab pulls up in front of the same restaurant Willow took me to a few days ago. I pay the driver and get out slightly confused, what was she doing here so early? I let her know I'm here and a moment later she opens the front doors. I glance at her, she's covered in more paint than she was a few days ago. Her hair is in a messy ponytail and there are streaks of paint on her face and all over her painting clothes.

"You're here!" She takes my hand excitedly and leads me to the basement.

I follow her confused but as soon as we get downstairs I understand. On the wall that was blank only two days ago, is a completed painting. Not just any painting, but a painting of something that resembles me. A profile of a woman with dark black hair and eyes closed with a huge smile covers the wall. There are hundreds of individually painted butterflies identical to the one that was on my nose yesterday. The woman on the wall has one on the tip of her nose, and a family of the following in a whirlwind across the other walls. The way Willow captured this moment and put it on the wall is nothing short of amazing.

"I got inspired yesterday and I came here and I couldn't stop painting until I was done. I only took breaks to drink coffee, but it was the moment yesterday. You had the butterfly on your nose and it sparked something in me. I have never been so inspired before." Willow rambles as I take it all in.

I'm careful this time as I walk closer to the painting. She painted me, on a wall, something that will be here forever. I was in absolute shock. I was worried she didn't like me and clearly, I was very very wrong. The paint glimmers in a way that tells me parts of it are still very wet so I don't touch it, but I get close. I can feel Willow's eyes on me waiting for me to say something but I am genuinely speechless.

"This is amazing." I finally say turning around.

Willow lets out a breath of relief and I smile. I walk toward her and kiss her. I know she's covered in paint but I don't care as I press my body into hers and kiss her as much as I can. I want to be as close to her as possible. This is seriously the nicest thing anyone has ever done for me. I kiss her for a few moments until I pull back.

"I need to take your photo." I look into her eyes and touch her cheek.

She nods and walks over to the mural. She poses in her usual fashion, smiling, making faces, looking adorable and beautiful all at once. Then she poses on the opposite side of the painting of me, touching the cheek just as she has many times to me. I snap a final photo, put my camera down and she runs into my arms. I kiss her and at this moment, I am thankful I went on this stupid trip.

Chapter Ten
One Month Later...

I pack up the last of my things. Some into the suitcase I plan to bring with me, but most of it into the truck on its way to the storage unit I bought. I knew I could only bring the essentials and that was easier than I thought it would be. I pick up the last box and walk outside to the truck.

"Here let me help," Nick appears from the other side of the truck and puts the last box in.

"All ready?" Sarah asks from the curb. She and Leah were sitting in the grass soaking up the sun and sipping on lemonades.

"I think so." They hop up and hug me before heading to the car.

Sarah was with me driving the truck while Nick and Leah were following in the car behind us. The storage unit was only ten minutes away and then we would be unpacking most of what I own. I hop in the passenger side while Sarah starts the truck.

"Do you have to go?" She's been asking me this since I told her I was going. After leaving Paris I decided to forgo my internship and apartment in the city to travel instead.

"You know I have to."

Those short days I spent with Willow truly opened my eyes and made me realize how much I want to see the world. I was going to use my savings but the craziest thing happened; I got a job offer in Ireland. Sarah posted one of the photos I took of Willow and her mural and it went viral, like millions of likes and comments virally. Everyone loved the painting as much as the photo I took of it, so I landed a short job in Ireland taking photos of small businesses and weddings and a variety of jobs. Once I finished there I had some things set up in Amsterdam, Australia, and Greece. Since I didn't know if or when I'd be back in the states, I decided to put most of my stuff in storage.

"But what about me? And how can you be my maid of honor from halfway across the world?" She laughs. I know this is her way of saying she'll miss me.

We all graduated a few weeks ago, and soon they would be starting their careers. Sarah and Nick were moving in together while Leah was moving to the city to start a new job. Leah and Tyler never got back together after Paris. Despite his attempts at making things right, she didn't take him back. Instead, she enjoyed the rest of our trip and broke up with him for good. The rest of us haven't seen him since graduation, we all debated keeping in touch but it wasn't exactly easy when Leah was still so close to us.

"I will be back in a heartbeat for your wedding, you know that," I reassure her. They hadn't even chosen a date yet, but I promised I would hop a last-minute flight if needed, to be there.

"Okay, okay you should check my phone I think the Willow photo is getting more likes again. I had to shut off my notifications."

I pick up her phone to look and sure enough, the photo is trending again. It gained both of us a huge following almost overnight and the photo still gets attention. I smile looking at the photo Willow's soft features steal the attention of the mural, which is a masterpiece in itself.

Willow and I surprisingly kept in touch after I left Paris. She ended up with new jobs due to her mural's sudden popularity too. Shortly after we left Paris she ended up in Spain just like she planned, sending me some murals she did. She said her mural of me got so much attention that she's often asked to incorporate butterflies into her new ones. We always say we'll try to meet up again, but part of me hopes 'we' stay in Paris. Some things are better left unfinished. I cried when she brought me to the airport that last day. I almost didn't get on that flight, wanting to explore the world with her. But I did and despite thinking of her most days, she changed my life.

When I got back home I secretly got a new tattoo. I had a few and they were all thought out and planned long before I even made the appointment. But this time I got off the flight home and the very next day I walked into the nearest tattoo shop. My friends don't know it yet, but I got a tattoo of a butterfly behind my ear. It serves as a small reminder that the trip to Paris I wish I didn't go on, ended up changing my life.

EPILOGUE
3 YEARS LATER...

"I can't believe you're getting married!" I run into Sarah's arms with a huge smile on my face.

"It's about damn time," Leah laughs.

"We wanted to wait until we graduated." Sarah rolls her eyes at us. She was the most adult of the three of us, even now.

"Was your flight okay?" Leah asks me.

"Yes, a little long, but I'm used to it now." The eight-hour flight from Spain was nothing compared to the eighteen hour one I took a few years ago to Australia. My passport definitely had gotten its money's worth.

"Miss world traveler is back?" Nick comes out holding a box of flowers. Sarah and Nick were set to get married tomorrow night, at a venue close to Sarah's childhood home in Eternal Port Valley.

"Nick!" He puts the box down and gives me a big hug. It makes me nostalgic for all the things I've missed with my best friends. I had been back home a few times over the last few months to help with wedding prep. I took my job as maid of honor seriously.

"Glad to have the gang back together," he smiles. It's unspoken that we don't mention Tyler anymore, for Leah's sake.

"The gang is about to be old and married," Leah teases.

"Oh, come on, we're the same age!" Sarah protests.

"Yes, but we still get to dance to single ladies at weddings." Leah says with a laugh.

"I don't know if that's something to brag about," I chuckle.

"I'll catch up with you all later. I have to get these to the place before it closes." Nick says, heading out the door.

Nick and Sarah's house was exactly what you'd expect from them. It was big enough for them and a few kids, which we all knew they wanted. It had a literal white picket fence and was in a small town. I mean, they only had one grocery store in like a twenty-mile radius. It wasn't what I'd want, but then again, I was as far away from settling down as possible.

"So, seeing anyone new?" Sarah asks, as if reading my mind.

"Nope, not anyone special, anyway." I shrug. There had been a few one-night stands, but no one was worth bringing home. Not in a long time, anyway.

"What about you, missy? You're very quiet." Sarah raises a brow at Leah.

"No way. I'm looking for someone at the wedding."

"Just please don't hit on any of my married family members," Sarah warns.

"Yeah, I don't need a repeat of your engagement party." Leah laughs.

"I'm surprised you're not freaking out more." I say to Sarah.

"Why would I freak out?"

"Because you're getting married tomorrow and you're high-strung."

"I'll say it, we thought you'd be going full Bridezilla on us." Leah adds.

"Oh stop, Nick and I are excited to get married, but we don't expect everything to go perfectly."

Leah and I share a knowing look. We'd be on high alert tomorrow to make sure everything went perfectly for our best friend.

"You look beautiful," Leah and I say in unison. Sarah's wedding dress shaped beautifully over her tall frame, melting to her curves modestly. It was entirely *her*.

"Thank you. I'm so glad you're both here." She holds our hands tight with a smile.

"We're here! I'm sorry we're late!" Sarah's older sister Alexandria and her son Elijah come in a hurry.

"It's okay, you're dressed so technically you're ready." Sarah laughs. Man, marriage really was chilling her out.

"Elijah is all ready, but Eden's outside with the baby. She was fussy last night, so she's napping right now. She'll be up and happy for the wedding time." Alexandria says with a smile. I'd only met her a few times, but she had always intimidated me. Alexandria was Sarah's bisexual sister who had a baby with her best friend and then married the female love of her life, Eden, and had another child with her. She was living the bisexual dream.

"Hi Eli," Sarah says to her nephew. He was the cutest seven years old I'd ever seen wearing a suit.

"Hi Auntie Sarah, congrats on the wedding," he smiles.

"Thanks buddy," she kisses his head.

"Can you two go make sure everyone's ready for us?" Sarah asks Leah and I. We nod and head outside to check with her mom. Everyone's waiting for us so we turn right around to get Sarah.

I was walking down the aisle with one of Nick brother's. He was on the quieter side, but at least he wasn't trying to hit on me. Nick's other brother, Charles, had a tendency to flirt with me when he was a few drinks in. Leah had offered to walk down the aisle with him since she knew how to shut down his flirting.

It was a traditional wedding with a white archway and parents walking the bride and groom down the aisle. There was a pastor who delivered the extra long service and by the end, my feet were killing me for standing so long in these heels. Sarah had done us a huge justice by letting us choose our bridesmaids' dresses, but she had insisted on the heels. Something my doc martens' loving feet were not used to. Sarah and Nick's wedding would be the last time I subjected myself to this torture. After the ceremony, we head to the reception hall, where I take off my heels almost immediately. *Lots of people took their shoes off at weddings. Would anyone even notice?*

"Same old Brooke, huh? Where are your Doc Martens?" A familiar voice says from behind me. But as I turn around, my eyes widen.

"Willow! What are you doing here?" A smile creeps across my cheeks and my arms fall around her.

"Sarah and Nick hired me to paint them." Willow looks the same, but different. Her blonde hair was just as messy and out of place, but there wasn't a speck of paint on her. She was wearing a short, light blue cocktail dress with a pair of brand new Doc Martens.

"Paint them what?" I ask, confused. *Sarah and Nick knew she was here and didn't tell me?*

"Them, I paint couples on their wedding day to commemorate the day. I don't do it too often but when Nick reached out and said it was a gift for Sarah, I knew I couldn't say no." She explains.

"That's so amazing," somehow words were failing me. There was so much I wanted to know and ask, but I couldn't get the words out.

"How are you? Are you living home again?" Willow and I had kept in touch after I left Paris for a few months, but over time and the changing time zones, we had lost touch. Sometimes I'd stalk her Instagram and wonder if we were in the same place, but we never crossed paths. *Until now.*

"I just got back from Spain, I was doing a few month project there. I have a bit of a break until my next project so I was going to stay with Leah."

"That's great! I should get started, but we should definitely catch up more before I leave again," she winks and the butterflies swarm my stomach.

"Okay," I nod. It was years later and she could still leave me speechless.

Leah walks over with a handful of drinks for us. "Did I just see Willow? Like Willow from Paris?"

"Yeah, I guess Nick hired her to paint the wedding." I say, but I don't believe it. There's no way they'd track down Willow and not tell me if there wasn't more to it. Of course, it wasn't like I could confront him about it during his wedding.

AFTER DANCING for hours and escaping Charles' advances, I notice Willow working away. The paintbrush doesn't leave the canvas, as she makes small delicate strokes. She's across the venue off to the side. She's gotten quite a crowd forming around her but she's too in her element to notice them. I wonder if she's painting what she's seeing or painting something specific from memory.

Sarah and Nick are dancing, a slow song I've never heard, but Sarah's head is on his chest and they both look peaceful. Some other couples are dancing, with a few of the kids running between them. Leah escaped to the bathroom when one of Sarah uncles asked her to dance, leaving me at the singles table alone.

Suddenly I can feel eyes on me, and a dread fills my stomach with knots. It's that terrible feeling where you know someone's watching you, but you have no idea who. So I try to casually glance around the room, but I stop when I see who it is. Willow has the paintbrush behind her ear, and she's staring right at me. She waves a hand, beckoning me over and I point to my chest with a brow raised. She nods and I weave between the people to walk across the room to her.

"What do you think? Will they like it?" Willow points at the canvas and again she's left me speechless.

The painting was of Nick and Sarah's first kiss. Something I didn't even realize she was here for, and must have painted from memory. She got all the minor details correct, and they looked lifelike. I knew Sarah was going to love it.

"They'll love it," I say aloud.

"Are you sure? He was vague."

"Yes, you captured their essence. They will both love it." I nod, not taking my eyes off it.

"I had to start over at first because I was painting you by mistake," she points to the canvas face down on the floor next to her.

"You did?" I can't hide the excitement in my voice.

"I didn't get very far, but yeah." She blushes softly.

We're interrupted by a string of people telling Willow how amazing the painting is. I walk back to the table, letting her get her praise. Part of me wanted to stay, see where the night could take us, but that was silly. It had been years. Surely she didn't see me in the same ways.

"How's it feel?" Sarah whispers, creeping up behind me.

"What?"

"Seeing her again," she says, as if it's obvious.

"Did you and Nick plan this?"

"No, I mean Nick did in hiring her. And I think because we all want to see you happy, but we planned nothing other than her painting for our wedding." Sarah explains.

"Uh huh," I nod, unconvinced.

"Did it bring up any old feelings?"

"Hey married lady, not everyone needs to be paired up."

"I know, but if there's someone out there for you, why fight it?" She shrugs. Nick steals her for a dance a few minutes later, leaving me to think over her words.

Sarah's words hang over my head as I sip the champagne. It's a while later, Nick and Sarah were leaving for their honeymoon and the guests were trickling out the door. Leah was flirting with one groomsman, but it was Willow who caught my eye. She was packing up her supplies, and it left me wondering if I'd ever see her again, *again*. Sarah had literally jumped for joy when she saw the painting, kissing Nick happily, that he surprised her. Willow had smiled in my direction, grateful I was right.

"Go on, you know you want to." Leah says stumbling over.

"What would be the point? It's just for one night."

"Sex," Leah says with a shrug.

"Leah!" I wasn't exactly a prude, but Willow wasn't just a one-night stand to me.

"I'll see you tomorrow roomie," Leah heads off with a different groomsman, who I'm pretty sure was who she was told to stay away from. But that's not my business.

Saying goodbye, I glance back at Willow, but her space is empty. Well, there you go. It clearly made my choice for me. Grabbing my purse, I head out to the parking lot. Hopefully, there were Uber's in this small ass town. Now attempting to find a signal in this town was another story. I hold up my phone and walk around in circles, back in these stupid heels.

"Need a ride somewhere?" Willow chimes from behind me.

"Willow? I thought you left." A smile takes up my entire face as I see hers.

"Look, there's something I wanted—"

I cut her off with a kiss. I didn't care if it was for one night or for a thousand. I wanted to remember what her lips felt like on mine. They were softer than I remembered, with the taste of cherry chapstick turning this into a cliche. Her hands grasp my waist, pulling hers into mine. She pulls back just for a second to look at me, biting her bottom lip. A smile crosses both of our faces and she kisses me this time, our teeth knocking together.

"Do you want to—"

"Yes," I nod furiously. Whatever it was, the answer was yes. I didn't want to lose her again.

"Come back to my hotel," she finishes.

"Oh, yes." I blush. It wasn't as if she hadn't seen me before, but this felt different.

Willow takes my hand, leading me back into the venue. We don't speak the entire way up to her room; the anxiety pouring off the both of us. Was this the same as before? Was it different? Part of me didn't want to know. The second she opens the door, we throw our stuff down on the table. Then her hands are back on my waist as she stands behind me. Willow pushes my hair off my shoulder and nibbles on my neck softly. I close my eyes, leaning back into her.

"You're so beautiful," she whispers. Her fingers dance down my arms, catching the thin fabric of my dress between of her fingers.

"Come here," she pulls me toward the bed and I expect her to push me back, but as she ducks down, I'm at a loss.

"What?"

"Those must be killing you." She grabs my heels and flings them across the room. Subsequently, she grabs one foot and massages it with the perfect amount of pressure. I'd marry her right here, right now if I wasn't worried she'd think I have a foot fetish.

"That feels wonderful," I smile.

"This is nothing," Willow winks and ducks under my dress, pulling my panties down my legs with her teeth. I could not possibly be more turned on, and she had barely touched me. Her head is beneath my dress, my legs hanging over her shoulders as she starts to kiss my inner thighs. Open, wet mouth kisses with a tiny nibble on the way to my core.

"Fuck," I groan as her mouth makes contact. I can feel her smile against me.

Willow licks my core dangerously slow, but just as I'm about to speak up she picks up the pace. Her tongue diving into me, it's her fingers that surprise me as she slips two inside me with a loud gasp. I grab my breast. Suddenly, all of my nerves lit up at once. I throw my head back as she starts a pattern of licking and pumping her fingers just close enough to make me beg.

"Please, faster," I say breathlessly, closing my thighs against her cheeks. I wasn't sure how she could breathe under there, but I didn't care. I wanted to cum, and I wanted to scream her name when I did it. As if reading my mind, she licks my clit in the perfect way to have me seeing stars.

"OH WILLOW!" I scream louder than intended.

"God, that was hot," Willow climbs onto the bed, sliding the zipper down the side of her dress and letting it melt into the floor.

"You're hot," I blush. She wipes her mouth against the back of her hand casually.

"So are you," Willow leans back into the pillows. Her perky breasts and lace panties, catching my attention.

"We're not done," I look at her.

"Oh?" she smirks.

"We're just getting started," I climb on top of her. We had too much lost time to make up for.

WILLOW and I lay tangled in the satin hotel sheets as the sunrise beats in on us. We'd been together for hours, only leaving the bed for Willow to grab something she assured me I'd love. Which, after three more orgasms, I can say I definitely do. My hair is surely a mess from the hairspray and my makeup can't be doing much for me at this point, but Willow looks amazing. The sun beating on her pale skin, her blue eyes shining perfectly back at me.

"What are you thinking about?" I ask. She had been quiet for too long. I had never been one of those girls who bugged their partner, but in this moment I genuinely wanted to know.

"You, this bed, life." She says mysteriously. It was obvious what she was thinking though, it was the same thing I was. *What would happen when we left this bed?*

"Hmm," I muse.

"Do you ever wonder what would've happened if we hadn't left Paris?" She asks with her eyes on me.

"Yes, all the time." I don't hesitate. There was no reason to lie to her.

Willow didn't speak for a long time. Her silence should scare me, but it doesn't. This situation was one neither of us could've expected. I never thought I'd see her again, and definitely not have been in her bed.

"Why don't we go back?"

"What? Where?"

"Paris."

"What are you saying?"

"Look, I've spent years looking for someone even a fraction as amazing as you. We both spend our lives nomadically, but why can't we do that together?"

I hesitate. *Was this just the after sex haze?* Who cares if it was? Willow was here, asking to be with her.

"You want to be together?" I clarify.

"Yes, as long as we can keep traveling. I'd love to spend my life seeing the rest of the world with you." Willow looks at me expectantly, so I kiss her. A softer one than before, a silent yes.

"Was that a yes?" She chuckles as we pull apart.

"YES!"

"Where are we going first?" She tangles her hands in mine.

"Back to Paris," I decide, thankful my best friend got married in the spring. It would be the same as we left it, except this time we'd leave it together.

Keep reading for a sneak peek...

SNEAK PEEK OF ONLY FOR THE SUMMER

I swear today has been one of the worst days of my life. I walk into my apartment, thankful to be home. It had been one thing after another all day long.

I was home from work over two hours late. My last appointment, which was supposed to be a quick haircut, had turned into someone deciding they wanted to go platinum blonde from dark brown. Before that, I had two cancellations and one kid who screamed the entire time. Oh, and this morning, I woke to my girlfriend breaking up with me over text. It was safe to say this day couldn't get any worse.

I kick off my sneakers by the front door, throw my bag on the floor, and plop on the couch. I'm too tired to make it the other twenty feet to my bedroom. I open my phone and re-read the texts Haley sent me.

Haley: *I'm sorry, but I can't do this anymore.*

Haley: *Until you figure out your feelings for Sienna or remove her from your life, I can't be in yours.*

Haley: *I'm sorry. I can't be anyone's second choice.*

I sigh and throw my phone across the couch and fall back into the pillows. I put one over my face and let out a muffled scream. This wasn't the first time a girlfriend of mine had an issue with my close friendship with Sienna. We had been best friends for years, so we were close. I just don't know why people have such a hard time accepting that we're *just* friends.

I've been down this road too many times to try to plead with Haley. If she wanted to break up over it, then fine. I was tired of having to defend my friendship. Eventually, the right girl would come around, someone who understood Sienna and I are just friends.

RING! RING! RING!

My phone rings from across the couch. I lift the pillow slightly and glance toward my phone. I see my brother's face on my screen and get up to answer it. Before Sienna, my best friend was and always has been my older brother Daniel. I hadn't told him about me and Haley, yet so he must just be calling to talk.

"Kenny!" Daniel says excitedly. He's the only one who gets away with calling me Kenny, a nickname I usually despise.

"Yes, Danny?"

"I'm engaged!" he all but shouts.

"What?!" I shoot up, sitting up straight. Did I hear him correctly or had the screaming done some hearing damage?

"I'm engaged! I proposed last night, but you're the first one I wanted to tell."

"Holy shit, this is amazing!" I force myself to say. Part of me is concerned about how quickly this is happening. I mean he hadn't been dating her for very long. This was completely unexpected.

"We're having an engagement party, can you come this weekend for a visit? I'd love you to meet her," he says a little more seriously.

"This weekend?" I ask surprised. There go my plans of soaking another breakup in ice cream and alcohol.

"Yeah, we want the families to meet. I know it's last minute, but it would mean a lot if you came." I can hear Holly whispering in the background.

"I, uh, I'll have to get someone to cover the shop." I don't know why I'm stalling, of course, I'd do anything to be home this weekend.

"And bring Haley too! We'd love to meet her," he says, unknowingly sending a sucker punch to my gut.

"We umm... broke up..." my voice cracks as I say it aloud for the first time.

"Fuck, hold on." I can hear the ocean in the background, and I know he must have walked onto the beach to talk to me alone. "Kenny, talk to me."

"I'm okay Danny, she had a problem with Sienna. I can't change her mind about it, so that's that. Let me go, I can make a call and see if someone can cover the shop for the weekend. I need to meet this new sister of mine," I add playfully.

"Let me know when you're coming in, I'll get you from the airport." He doesn't push the Haley situation further.

We say our goodbyes and I immediately make a second phone call. She picks up on the second ring with a sing-song hello.

"Wanna come over?" I groan. Originally I was going to go for a run, run out my problems and try to salvage my mood.

"You sound like crap, do you want pizza or Chinese?" That's what I love about Sienna, her blunt and bitter honesty.

"Pizza, with pepperoni and mozzarella sticks and buffalo wings. Oh, and a cannoli,"

"Terrible day order, I got it. Give me like thirty."

THIRTY MINUTES later Sienna is standing on my doorstep holding a pizza, a bag of food, and a smile. A smile I swear could cure the worst of bad days. She slips her shoes off as I grab the food from her and bring it to the small island in my kitchen.

"So you gonna tell me what caused the terrible day order? I swear I've only ordered this like twice before." Sienna slips onto the couch, I walk over a plate of food and a glass of water for her.

"Haley broke up with me," I say holding my breath.

"What a bitch," she mumbles, a mouth full of food.

"Did she say why?" This was a commonly asked question.

"No, she just said it, uh wasn't working anymore," I lie. I didn't want to bring up the real reason. Knowing Sienna, she'd feel terrible and blame herself.

I don't say anything else while I slide beside her on the couch after grabbing the remote. We put on some shitty reality tv, the only sounds are the couples fighting and the chewing of our food.

"Daniel's getting married," I try to add casually.

"WHAT?! How did you not lead with that?" She squeals.

"He's having an engagement party this weekend, he told me to bring Haley but now we're over so I guess I'm going stag."

Before Sienna comes over, I had manage to get Christine to cover the shop for the week. I haven't been home in months, and I know my parents will appreciate an extended trip. Running my own business has many perks but in times like this, I'm thankful for my staff. I couldn't leave for a week on my own without knowing I can trust my assistant manager to handle everything.

"Why don't you take me?" Sienna asks, smiling.

"W-What?" I almost choke on my pizza.

"What? I'm off for the summer. I've already met Daniel. I'm due for a vacation," she says like it's no big deal.

"You want to go?" I ask, surprised.

"Why wouldn't I?" she counters, raising an eyebrow.

"My family will be asking about my girlfriend, and I'll have to give them the whole '*I just got dumped*' speech and see their pity," I groan. It's bad enough hearing it in Danny's voice.

"What if you didn't?" Her green eyes are gleaming. Then my best friend proceeds to tell me what might be the craziest thing we've ever done.

ALSO BY SHANNON O'CONNOR

ONLY IN SEASIDE SERIES

(each book can be read as a standalone)

Only the Beginning

Only for the Summer

Only for Revenge

Only for the Baby

Only Convenient

Only for the Holidays

Only Friends

ETERNAL PORT VALLEY SERIES

(each book can be read as a standalone)

Unexpected Departure

Unexpected Days

ETERNAL PORT VALLEY UNIVERSITY

(each novella can be read as a standalone)

Freshman Fever

Out Played

EPU#3

EPU#4

STANDALONES

Electric Love

Butterflies in Paris

All's Fair in Love & Vegas

I Saw Mommy Kissing the Nanny

ANTHOLOGIES

A Taste Of You

Because I F*cking Said So

Hot Boy Summer

Girls Just Wanna Have Fundamental Rights

Evil Queen: Vol II

An Appetite for You

Misfires at Midnight

Personal Foul

POETRY

For Always

Holding on to Nothing

Say it Everyday

Midnights in a Mustang

Five More Minutes

When Lust Was Enough

Isolation

All of Me

Lost Moments

Cosmic

About the Author

Shannon O'Connor is a twenty-something, bisexual, self-published poet of several books and counting. She released her first novel, *Electric Love* in 2021 and is currently working on several sapphic romance novels. She believes there is a lack of positive Female/Female romances in the world, and wants to make them more accessible. She is often found in coffee shops, probably writing about someone she shouldn't be.

Heat. Heart. & A Bit of Both.

Check out more work & updates on: